LITTLE RED

BY BARRY HUTCHISON
& MARK PEARCE

Titles in Once Upon *Another* Time…

Badger Publishing Limited
Oldmedow Road,
Hardwick Industrial Estate,
King's Lynn PE30 4JJ

 Badger
LEARNING

Telephone: **01438 791037**
www.badgerlearning.co.uk

2 4 6 8 10 9 7 5 3

Little Red
ISBN 978-1-78464-522-9

Text © Barry Hutchison 2016
Complete work © Badger Publishing Limited 2016

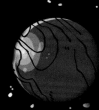

CONTENTS

CHARACTERS

TTLE RED

PROFESSOR T

JOLLAX

VOCABULARY

deliver

facility

gobbled

inventions

offload

orbiting

squirmed

supplies

thrusters

uneasy

Once Upon A Time...

ANOTHER

CHAPTER ONE

GRANDMA'S HOUSE

"This is supply ship Delta, looking for permission to land," said Little Red into her microphone.

Her spacecraft was orbiting around a small forest moon.

Down below, she could see the research station she had been sent to deliver supplies to.

Grandma's House was the best cake-research facility in the galaxy.

"Hi Delta," crackled a voice over her headset. "Permission granted. Welcome to Grandma's House."

Little Red's pointed ears twitched happily.

Her ship had been followed by an alien spacecraft for a few thousand miles and she had been worried she would be attacked.

The ship had vanished, though, and it looked like the mission would go smoothly after all.

After landing the ship, Little Red loaded the supplies onto the transport trolley.

Strange-looking workers led her to the docking bay entrance before returning to their duties.

A moment later, the door slid open. A man in a white coat gave Little Red a friendly wave.

She waved back but there was something odd about him.

She knew this was Professor T, one of the station's cake scientists. He looked different to the hologram she had been shown, though.

"What a big nose you have," she blurted, then she gasped. "Sorry, that was so rude."

The professor smiled strangely. "No harm done," he said. "This way."

As he turned, Little Red got a good look at the prof's nose. It was massive. She was surprised he hadn't smelled her coming.

CHAPTER TWO
BIG EYES

In the storage area, Little Red hurried to offload the supplies.

The smell of baking and buttercream icing was making her hungry.

Another scientist was watching her. Little Red recognised her as Jollax, the lizard-like alien in charge of developing new cake flavours.

She was the genius behind tuna-flavoured icing, and had won awards for her cake-based inventions.

Just as with Professor T, something looked odd about Jollax.

"What big eyes you have," Little Red remarked.

Jollax blinked. "All the better to sssssseeeee you with," she hissed, then she slipped into the shadows and disappeared.

Little Red shuddered. This place was getting weirder by the second.

With her cargo offloaded, Little Red hopped aboard the transport trolley and guided it towards the exit.

The sooner she was back on her ship, the happier she would be.

As she got near the exit, she saw it had been blocked by Professor T and Jollax.

There were other crew members there, too. Their ears were even bigger than Little Red's. The way they all stared at her made her very uneasy.

The trolley beeped as Little Red backed up. "Uh... I'll find another way out," she said. "I can see you guys are busy being, um, really scary."

With a high-pitched scream, the scientists charged. Little Red hopped off the transport wagon and ran as fast as she could.

She ducked down corridors. She dodged through labs.

No matter how fast she ran, though, the scientists were never far behind.

"Back off, guys," she called. "I d-don't want to hurt you!"

Back along the corridor, she heard the scientists snigger.

Stumbling around a corner, Little Red spotted a door. "Cleaning cupboard," she whispered, reading the sign. "A hiding place!"

Pulling the door open, Little Red gasped. Two scientists squirmed on the floor, their hands tied behind their backs.

"It arrived j-just before you did," stammered the real Professor T. "It tricked us. It wants all the chocolate sprinkles!"

Suddenly, two figures lurched around the bend.

A moment ago, they had looked like strange versions of the scientists but now they were more like living putty.

The jelly-like shapes squished together to form one wobbly creature. "A shape-shifter," Little Red said. "Of course."

CHAPTER THREE
BIG TEETH

The blob opened, revealing huge, scary fangs. "Like our teeth?" it hissed. "All the better to eat you with."

"They're big," Little Red admitted.

Then, with a roar, she seemed to explode.

"*ROARRRR!*"

She doubled in size, then doubled again.

Arms and eyes and floppy tentacles grew from her body.

The shape-shifter let out a gasp as Little Red opened her jaws wide and gobbled it up.

With a **BURP!** Little Red returned to her normal size and shape.

"But mine are bigger."

After releasing the scientists, Little Red returned to her ship and blasted off, armed with a year's supply of free cake.

As she left orbit, her radio crackled. "Come in, Little Red, this is base. We need you to deliver some building supplies to three pig-people on planet Pork."

An alien's work is never done! Little Red smiled.

Then she hit the thrusters and zoomed off towards her next adventure.

STORY FACTS

The idea for *Little Red* came from a couple of 'firsts' of mine. The story of Little Red Riding Hood is the first fairy tale I remember scaring me when I was very young, and the film *Alien* was the first scary movie I ever saw. Mashing the two of them together seemed like a great way to kick off a story.

I didn't want just any old monster, though, and knew that the villain of *Little Red* had to be something special. The idea of alien shapeshifters has always worried me. What if your teacher wasn't really your teacher, or your best friend was something else in disguise? It would be terrifying! And so, the alien in *Little Red* was born.

Looking for more shapeshifting aliens?
Check out *Charlie and the Great Glass Elevator*, a book by Roald Dahl, which features a gang of scary shapeshifters called the Vermicious Knids.

QUESTIONS

Where is this story set?
(page 6)

What was Little Red delivering?
(page 14)

Who stopped her from leaving?
(page 18)

Where were the real Professor T and Jollax being held?
(page 20)

Were you surprised at Little Red's secret?

MEET THE AUTHOR

Barry Hutchison lurks in the mountains of the Highlands of Scotland, making up random nonsense, then writing it all down.

His biggest fear is that someone will someday discover how much fun his job is and immediately put a stop to it. His second biggest fear is squirrels.

MEET THE ILLUSTRATOR

Mark Pearce is an illustrator and comic artist from Bristol. His career as a WWE wrestler didn't quite work out on account of his fear of chairs.

He likes shooty computer games, bad films and cheeseburgers.

32